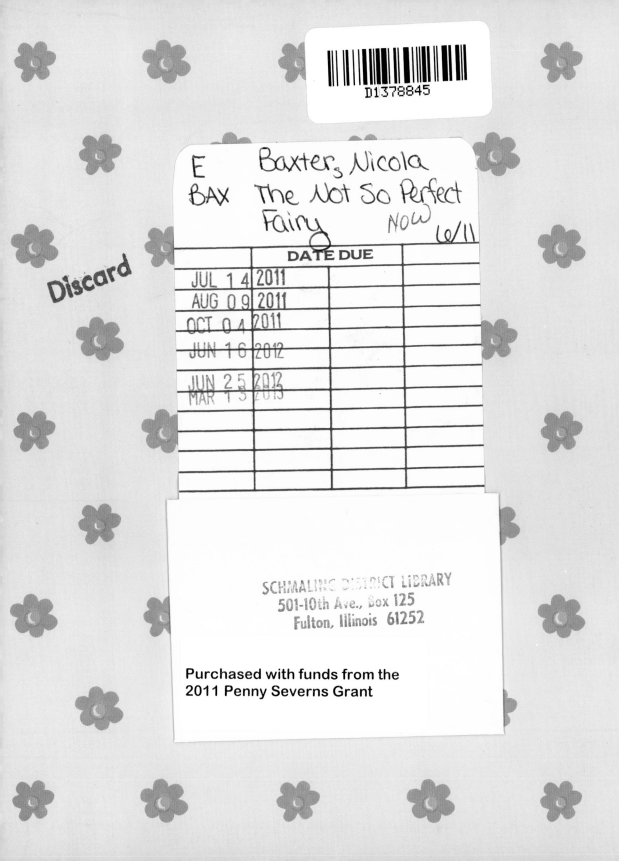

D1378845

This edition is published by
Armadillo,
an imprint of Anness Publishing Ltd,
Hermes House,
88–89 Blackfriars Road,
London SE1 8HA;
tel. 020 7401 2077;
fax 020 7633 9499
www.annesspublishing.com

© Anness Publishing Ltd 2004, 2010

Trees are being cultivated to
replace the materials used
to make this product. For further
information about our ecological
investment scheme, go to
www.annesspublishing.com/trees

Produced for Anness Publishing Ltd
by Nicola Baxter
Illustrator: Daniel
Howarth/Advocate
Designer: Amanda Hawkes

PUBLISHER'S NOTE
Although the advice and
information in this book are
believed to be accurate and true
at the time of going to press,
neither the authors nor the
publisher can accept any legal
responsibility or liability for any
errors or omissions that may have
been made.

Starting to read – it's perfect!

This delightful story helps to make sharing
books with your child successful and enjoyable.
The simple, repeated language and vibrant
characters make it ideal to help with your
child's first steps in reading.

The book can be used in several ways to help
your child gain confidence. You could start
by reading the illustrated words at the edge
of each left-hand page with your child.

All the words on the right-hand page have already
appeared on the left-hand page, so have fun
trying to spot the same words in the story itself.

Finally, all the illustrated words can be found
at the end of the book, so you and your child
can enjoy looking at them together.

The not so Perfect Fairy

Written by Nicola Baxter · Illustrated by Pauline Siewert

ARMADILLO

fairy

granny

suitcase

mother

Little Fairy Fluff is very excited. She is going to stay with her granny.

She packs her suitcase with all the things she needs.

"Now I will pack it again with all the things you **really** need!" says her mother.

Her mother packs the suitcase.

house

stairs

bed

book

Fairy Fluff's mother takes her to Granny's house. It is not far away.

"How lovely to see you!" says Granny.

She takes Fairy Fluff up the stairs.

"This is your bed," she says.

There is a big book on the bed.

"Oh dear," says Granny. "I forgot that was there."

Granny takes the book away.

window

rain

shop

basket

The next day, Granny looks out of the window.

"Look at the rain!" she says. "Oh dear, I must go to the shop. You stay here, Fairy Fluff."

"I will put the breakfast things away for you," says Fairy Fluff.

Granny takes her basket and waves goodbye.

"I will only be a minute," she says.

Fairy Fluff waves out of the window.

plate

milk

chair

shelf

Fairy Fluff tries to tidy up. She is not careful.

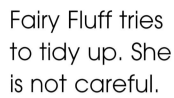

Oh dear! She drops a plate!

Oh dear! She spills the milk!

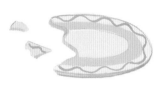

Oh dear! She knocks over a chair!

Oh dear! Oh dear! Oh dear! Fairy Fluff knocks down a shelf.

"What shall I do now?" says Fairy Fluff. "Look at Granny's house!"

Now Granny's house is not tidy!

wand

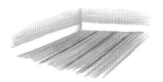

floor

shoes

clothes

Suddenly, Fairy Fluff sees the big book. It is a magic book!

"I could say a spell to tidy everything up," says Fairy Fluff. "I will need my wand."

The wand is in her suitcase. Fairy Fluff is in a hurry.

Oh dear! The suitcase falls on the floor! Out fall her shoes and her clothes.

"I will need to hurry to tidy up!"
says Fairy Fluff.

eyes

words

stars

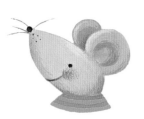

mouse

Fairy Fluff goes downstairs. She chooses a spell. She shuts her eyes. She waves her wand. She says the words in the book.

Magic stars appear. But Fairy Fluff has only just learnt to read.

The spell is for a clean, tidy house. Oh no! Fairy Fluff says a spell for a clean, tidy mouse!

Oh no! Fairy Fluff has a mouse!

sandwiches

cakes

cookies

dessert

Just then, Granny comes home. She sees all the mess.

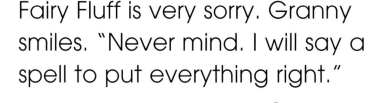

"Oh, Fairy Fluff," she says.

Fairy Fluff is very sorry. Granny smiles. "Never mind. I will say a spell to put everything right."

Soon it is lunchtime. Granny makes sandwiches, cakes, cookies and dessert!

The house looks lovely again. And the magic book has been hidden safely away!

Everything is all right again.

Picture dictionary

Now you can read these words!

basket

bed

book

cakes

chair

clothes

cookies

dessert

eyes

floor

granny

house

milk

mother

mouse

plate

rain

sandwiches

shelf

shoes

shop

stairs

stars

suitcase

wand

window

words